Maple Tree Farm
BOOK FOUR

Anna's Prize

Written by Katherine Rawson

Illustrated by Steven Petruccio

PIONEER VALLEY EDUCATIONAL PRESS, INC.

Chapter 1

Blackberry Pie

Anna stood anxiously in front of the
hot black stove with her fingers crossed.
"Oh, I hope my pies turned out,"
she said as she opened the heavy oven door.
A warm, sweet aroma filled the kitchen
as Anna carefully lifted out
a steaming golden-crusted pie and
set it on the table. She stood back
to admire her creation.

Aunt Polly came over and inspected the pie.
"It looks magnificent," she said.

"Do you think it's good enough
to win a prize?" Anna asked nervously.

"It could," said Aunt Polly.
"You crimped the edge of the crust beautifully,
and it smells delicious.
Blackberries make a really good pie."

Sophie, Anna's young cousin, inched closer and gazed admiringly at the pie. "It's my favorite kind!"

"I really want to win a blue ribbon at the county fair tomorrow," said Anna.

Aunt Polly smiled. "Winning is nice," she said. "But, blue ribbon or not, I know this is one really wonderful pie."

"Can I taste?" asked Sophie,
  reaching for the pie.

"Don't touch!" snapped Anna,
  and Sophie quickly withdrew her hand.

"Sorry," said Anna, "but this pie
  is for the contest tomorrow.
  There's another one in the oven
  for us to eat. Suddenly, Anna clapped
  her hand over her mouth, exclaiming,
"Oh no! The other pie!"

The smell of burnt crust came pouring out
when Anna opened the oven door.
"It's ruined!" she cried,
setting the blackened pie on the table.

"Oh, dear," said Aunt Polly.
"It looks like you pushed it
too far toward the back of the oven."

"And then I left it in too long.
Oh, baking is so hard!" said Anna,
slumping down in a chair.

"The first pie is fine," said Aunt Polly soothingly,
"and we'll just feed this other one to the chickens."

Aunt Polly took a square woven basket
off the shelf and set the good pie inside it.
"See? You can carry it in this basket."
She covered the pie with a red-checkered cloth
napkin and closed the basket lid.
"Now it's all ready for tomorrow," she said
as she set the basket on the counter
and put the burnt pie next to it.

"But what pie are we going to eat?"
whined Sophie.

Aunt Polly hugged her.
"Don't you worry, little one.
We'll make more pies, just not today."

Chapter 2

I Hope I Win

Anna jumped up. "It's time to feed the chickens,"
she said, grabbing the bucket
of kitchen scraps that Aunt Polly
kept by the door. "Do you want to help, Sophie?"
she said to her little cousin.

Sophie followed her outside,
but halfway across the yard, Anna stopped.
"I forgot to bring
the burnt pie for the chickens.
Can you go back and get it?"

Sophie turned back
toward the house while Anna
continued to the barnyard.

Chickens clucked around her
as she threw out the scraps.
Anna smiled to herself, thinking
about all she had experienced
since she had arrived at Maple Tree Farm.
"I've learned to take care of chickens
and make ice cream and bake pies,
and now my pie is going to win a prize
at the fair. I just know it."

Anna was so busy with her thoughts
that she forgot about the burnt pie.
She didn't notice that Sophie
hadn't brought it out to the chicken yard.

The next morning, the family

got up before sunrise.

After breakfast, Uncle Al and Harry

hitched the horses to the wagon

and the family piled in.

Sophie wanted to carry the pie basket,

but Anna held it tightly on her lap.

She wanted to safeguard her precious creation herself.

She didn't notice that Sophie drew in a sharp breath

as Anna lifted the basket lid and peeked inside.

"All safe and sound," said Anna,

  patting the cloth napkin.

As soon as the family arrived

at the fair, Anna went to drop off her pie.

She entered a long, low building

and walked past tables groaning

under the weight of jars of jam and pickles,

cakes, plates of cookies,

and colorful displays of vegetables.

Near the back, she spotted Mrs. Clyde,

who was in charge of the pies.

"Here's my pie," said Anna proudly,

handing over her basket.

Mrs. Clyde opened the lid

and lifted a corner of the napkin.

She regarded the pie for a moment with a frown.

"Are you sure this is the pie for the contest?"

"Yes!" exclaimed Anna. "I really, really

want to win," she added.

"Well, dear," said Mrs. Clyde,

patting Anna's shoulder, "winning isn't everything."

"I know," said Anna.

"But I still hope I do."

And she ran off to find her cousins.

Chapter 3
The Pie Contest

Uncle Al gave each of the children a few cents to spend as they liked. "We'll meet you by the pies at 4:00," he said. Then he and Aunt Polly went to see the cows and horses.

"Let's go to the merry-go-round," Anna proposed to her cousins.

"We can ride for a nickel." Harry agreed, but Sophie was silent.

Anna glanced down at her cousin with bewilderment. "Don't you like the merry-go-round?" she asked.

"Yes," said Sophie, but her face was glum.

Later that afternoon
after the children had ridden
the merry-go-round, admired the fair food,
and inspected the farm animal exhibits,
Anna said, "Let's see if they've finished
judging the pies."

The three cousins
headed for the low building,
but Sophie stopped at the entrance.

"What's the matter with you?" said Anna.
She grabbed Sophie's hand
and pulled the little girl inside with her.

At the pie table, Anna's eye fell

on a bright blue ribbon, and her heart

beat with excitement.

But the first-prize winner

was an apple pie, not blackberry like Anna's.

"Oh, well," she thought.

"Second or third place is good too."

But the red ribbon was on a peach pie

and the third-place pie wasn't Anna's either.

Then she saw it.

At the end of the table

sat a burnt pie.

Next to it was a tag with Anna's name

and the place where she lived: Maple Tree Farm.

Anna's jaw dropped.

"What happened to my pie?" she whispered

in disbelief.

Sophie looked up at her.

"I'm sorry," she said in a small voice.

"Sorry?" Anna's eyes narrowed. Her stomach knotted.

"Sorry for what?" Anna said through clenched teeth.

"I couldn't help it," sniffed Sophie
    as a tear ran down her cheek.

"I only meant to take a little bite,
    but it tasted so good that I couldn't stop."

"You took my pie!" shrieked Anna.

"I didn't mean to!" cried Sophie.

"And then you put the burnt pie

in the basket. Oh, how could you?"

Anna's face was bright red.

"My pie could have won a blue ribbon!

I know it could have. Now I've lost my chance

and all because of you. How could you, Sophie?"

Anna ran out of the building.

Chapter 4
A Blue Ribbon

All the way home from the fair,

Anna sat in the wagon

with her arms crossed and a scowl on her face.

She wouldn't speak to or even look at Sophie.

The next morning at breakfast it was the same.

When Sophie tried to follow her to the chicken coop,

Anna turned around and snarled at her,

"Stay away from me!"

After feeding the chickens, Anna sat glumly

on the back steps. Aunt Polly came and

sat down next to her.

"Sophie is just a little girl," she said,

putting her arm around Anna.

"But she's big enough to know better,"
complained Anna. She wistfully remembered
her hopes for the blue ribbon.
"She shouldn't have eaten my pie."

"You could see it as a compliment," suggested
Aunt Polly. "The pie was too good not to eat."

Anna considered this for a moment.
A glimmer of a smile
crossed her face.

"There will be other pies and other contests,"
Aunt Polly added.

"But I really wanted to win that one," Anna reminded
her aunt.

"I know." Aunt Polly was quiet for a minute.
"I think there are enough blackberries
left for one more pie," she said.
"We could make another one
if someone wanted to bake it."

"It's not the same as baking a prize-winning pie."

"Well, you think about it."
Aunt Polly went inside.

A few minutes later,

Anna heard the door behind her creak open.

Sophie came down the steps

and held out a folded piece of paper.

"For you," she said shyly.

"Oh!" said Anna when she unfolded
the paper and saw a drawing
of a big blue ribbon. Beneath the drawing,
Sophie had written, "Best Cousin."
Suddenly, the black cloud that had been hanging
over Anna all morning floated away.

"I had to ask Mama how to spell 'Cousin,'"
said Sophie, looking at her feet.
"I'm sorry you lost the blue ribbon because of me."

"It's alright," said Anna,
hugging the little girl.
"This one is even better.
'Best Cousin' is the greatest prize of all."

Sophie smiled.

"Do you want to help me bake another pie?" asked Anna. "Aunt Polly says we can."

"Blackberry?"

"Yes!" said Anna.

"It's my favorite kind," said Sophie.

"I know," laughed Anna.
  She held out her hand to her little cousin,
  and the two went inside to start baking.